Story Hour— Starring Megan!

Julie Brillhart

ALBERT WHITMAN & COMPANY, MORTON GROVE, ILLINOIS

Library of Congress Cataloging-in-Publication Data

Brillhart, Julie.
Story hour—starring Megan! / Julie Brillhart.
p. cm.
Summary: When Megan's mother, the
librarian, cannot read to the children
at a story hour, beginning reader Megan
takes over the job.
ISBN 0-8075-7628-X
[1. Books and reading—Fiction.]   1. Title.
PZ7.B7666St   1992
[E]—dc20   91-19523
                                        CIP
                                        AC

Text and illustrations © 1992 by Julie Brillhart.
Cover and interior design by Karen A. Yops.
Published in 1992 by Albert Whitman & Company,
6340 Oakton Street, Morton Grove, Illinois 60053-2723.
Published simultaneously in Canada by
General Publishing, Limited, Toronto.
All rights reserved. Printed in the U.S.A.
10 9 8 7 6 5 4 3 2 1

The illustrations are in pen and watercolor.
The typeface is Korinna.

TO THE HOLMES FAMILY AND THE E.P.L.

Once in awhile, when the sitter couldn't come, Megan and her baby brother, Nathan, got to spend an afternoon with their mother at the town library. Their mother was the librarian.

Megan liked the library because she had jobs to do.
Her mother called her the "assistant." She put away the
children's books and picked up the stuffed animals.

She decorated the bulletin board and watered the plants.

And when things got very, very busy,

Megan was always ready to help with Nathan.

But most of all, Megan liked the library because she loved books and was learning to read. She couldn't wait to read every book in the whole library!

Whenever she had a chance, Megan would curl up with *Fly up High* and try to sound out the words. Often she got stuck, and her mother would help her.

Megan would sigh. "Oh, reading is so hard!"

"I know," said her mother. "But keep trying. It will come."

So Megan kept on trying. She tried at school,

in the car,

at the supermarket,

in the bathtub,

after dinner,

and even after lights out!
She had never tried so hard at anything before.

One time the sitter couldn't come on the day Megan's mother had story hour. "I hope Nathan sleeps through the story," said Megan's mother as the children started to arrive.

Suddenly a stuffed dinosaur came flying through the book slot in the library door. "Oh, good!" said Megan. "Andrew's here!"

Andrew came in carrying a pile of dinosaur books. "Guess what?" said Megan. "I'm learning to read!"

"Oh," said Andrew. "Are there any new books with pteranodons?"

"No," said Megan. "And aren't you ever going to read about *anything* else?"

Megan led the group to the children's room and
passed out name tags. She helped the younger children
pin on their tags.

"Welcome to story hour," said Megan's mother. "Today
I would like to read—"

Right then Nathan let out a howl. Everyone turned to look.

"Just a minute," said Megan's mother. And she got up.

She tried everything to calm Nathan down, but he kept screaming.

The children were getting restless. "Please be patient,"
said Megan's mother. "I'm sure we will begin shortly."

While all this was going on, Megan sat thinking.
Suddenly she had a great idea!

She slipped away and ran to get her favorite book.

Megan sat down in front of all the children. She felt a little scared. "I would like to read *Fly up High*," she said.

Everyone looked at her in amazement. The room became very quiet, and Nathan even stopped crying. Megan began to read.

She read on and on. She showed the children the pictures, just the way her mother did. She got stuck on a few words, but she kept going. Nobody seemed to notice when she made a mistake.

She read the whole book!
The children all clapped and cheered. And so did some moms and dads who had come in. Megan felt terrific!

She looked over at her mom. "I did it!" Megan said.
"You sure did," said her mother. "And all by yourself!
I'm very proud of you!"

"I didn't know you could read THAT much," said
Andrew. "Can I borrow your book?"

Megan laughed. "Sure," she said. "But it's not about
dinosaurs!"

When everyone had gone, Megan's mother gave her a
big, big hug. "You were wonderful!" she said. "You saved
the day!"

"Yay!" said Megan. "Now I'll read every book in the
whole library!"

And she started right away.